The Kid and the Chameleon

Time to Read™ is an early reader program designed to guide children to literacy success regardless of age or grade level. The program's three levels correspond to stages of reading readiness, making book selection straightforward, and assuring that when it's time for a child to read, the right book is waiting.

Level 1

Beginning to Read

- Large, simple type
- Basic vocabulary
- Word repetition
- Strong illustration support

Level 2

Reading with Help

- Short sentences
- Engaging stories
- Simple dialogue
- Illustration support

Level 3

Reading Independently

- Longer sentences
- Harder words
- Short paragraphs
- Increased story complexity

Also by Sheri Mabry

The Kid and the Chameleon Sleepover
The Kid and the Chameleon Go to School

The Kid and the Chameleon

Sheri Mabry   illustrated by Joanie Stone

Albert Whitman & Company
Chicago, Illinois

For Whitnie, Kaiti, and Hailie: may you always be
blessed with beautiful friendships—SM

To John and Yvette—JS

Library of Congress Cataloging-in-Publication data is on file with the publisher.

Text copyright © 2019 by Sheri Mabry
Illustrations copyright © 2019 by Albert Whitman & Company
Illustrations by Joanie Stone
Hardcover edition first published in the United States of America
in 2019 by Albert Whitman & Company
Paperback edition first published in the United States of America
in 2019 by Albert Whitman & Company
ISBN 978-0-8075-4167-8 (paperback)
ISBN 978-0-8075-4175-3 (ebook)

Printed in China
10 9 8 7 6 5 4 3 2 1 WKT 24 23 22 21 20 19

Design by Morgan Beck

For more information about Albert Whitman & Company,
visit our website at www.albertwhitman.com.

100 Years of Albert Whitman & Company
Celebrate with us in 2019!

Chapter One

A chameleon sat on a leaf.

He looked down. He saw a kid.

A kid sat on a log.

She looked up. She saw a
chameleon.

"Look, I found you!" said the girl.

"I am not lost," said the chameleon.

"I'm Tessy," said the girl. "I'll name you Louie."

"I already have a name."
The chameleon's tongue flicked.
"It's Newton."

"What are you?" asked Tessy.

"I am a chameleon," said Newton.

"You look like a lizard," said Tessy.

"Same thing," said Newton. "But I prefer chameleon. It's a bigger word."

"What are you?"

"I am a kid!" said Tessy.

"You look like a human," said Newton.

"I am," said Tessy. "But kid humans are the most fun."

Tessy filled a jar with her favorites.

A ribbon.

A picture of her grandma.

A piece of gum.

"You'll love these!"

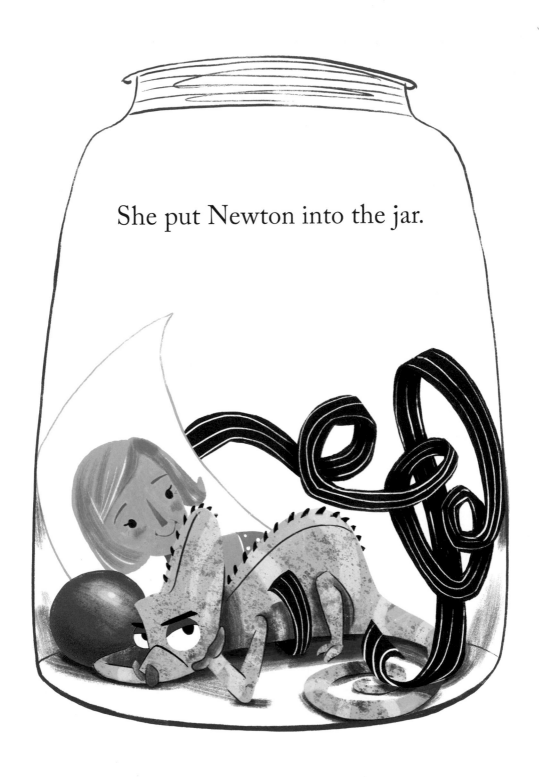

She put Newton into the jar.

He looked around.

No rock.

No soggy leaves.

No bugs.

"This is not chameleon stuff."

He crawled out. He climbed onto

a branch. "Jars are not

my thing."

"We can be friends, Louie,"
said Tessy.

"You are a kid. I am a chameleon.
I'm not making any promises,"
said Newton. "And call me Newton."

Chapter Two

Tessy picked Newton up. "We can have fun together! Let's have a picnic," she said.

"I was having fun," said Newton. "Please put me down. And what is a picnic?"

"You'll see," said Tessy.

She put out a sandwich.
She put out a cookie.
She put out a juice box.

Newton sat on the basket. He pointed his tail. "Hand me that," he said.

"The cookie?" asked Tessy. "Sorry. No cookies before you eat lunch."

"There are *rules* to a picnic?" said Newton. "I want the cricket not the cookie."

"Ew," said Tessy. "No crickets on a picnic. It is a kid rule."

"No making fun of what I eat," said
Newton. "That's not nice."

Tessy gave Newton the juice box.
"Have a sip of this."

Newton flicked his tongue out but
not in. "Ouch! My tongue is ssthuck!"

He pulled it back in. "I don't sip.
And I do *not* drink from straws,"
said Newton. "It is a chameleon rule."

Newton went into the basket. He shut one eye. He shut the other eye.

He was not having fun. He turned brown.

"Wait! Try this grape," said Tessy. She dropped it into the basket.

"Oww!" said Newton. "Grapes hurt. Picnics are not my thing."

Chapter Three

A chameleon sat on a rock.

And sat.

A kid sat on a rock.

And sat.

"What are we doing?" said Tessy.
"Rock sitting. You wanted to
have fun. I will show you fun,"
said Newton.

Tessy sat on her rock.

She sat.

She waited.

Finally she said, "When does the fun start?"

"What do you mean? It already started. We are in the middle of the fun," said Newton.

"Rock sitting is not fun," said Tessy.

"Then we will change colors," said Newton.

"I can't change colors," said Tessy, "unless I change my shoes, my socks, my shorts, my shirt, and my headband."

"That's a lot of work," said Newton. "Let's just change one color."

Newton shut his eyes.

"What are you doing?" asked Tessy.

"Thinking happy thoughts," said Newton. "That helps me change colors."

He thought of crickets.

He thought of raindrops.

He thought of sleep.

He smiled.

He turned orange.

Tessy wanted to try. She thought happy thoughts.

She thought of apples.

She thought of her grandma.

She thought of fun.

She smiled.

"Did I turn colors?" asked Tessy.

"No," said Newton. "Try again."

Tessy thought harder.

"Did I turn colors?" asked Tessy.

"No," said Newton. "Try again."

"This is not fun!" said Tessy. "I can't change colors! It's a kid rule. Let's go."

"I'm thinking," said Newton. "Shhhh."

"That is not nice!" said Tessy.

"It is nice if it keeps you quiet," said Newton.

Tessy clenched her fists. Her face turned red.

Newton opened one eye.
He opened the other eye.
"Yep," said Newton.
"Yep what?"
asked Tessy.

"Yep, it worked," said Newton. "You
changed colors."

"Changing colors is not fun!" Tessy
crossed her arms. "And rock sitting is
not my thing!"

Chapter Four

Tessy had a jumpy idea. She put Newton in her pocket.

Newton had a sleepy idea. He shut his eyes.

Tessy jumped. Newton popped out of her pocket.

Tessy jumped again. Newton popped out of her pocket again.

In! Out! In! Out!

"Jumping rope hurts my head!" he said.

"Jumping rope is fun!" said Tessy.
"I could do it all day!"

"Let's go swimming," said Newton.

"How can you jump over the same rope all day?" asked Newton. "When I jump over something, I keep on going."

"Swimming is fun!" said Tessy. "But there is no pool."

"Yes there is," said Newton. "Follow me."

Newton walked slowly. Tessy followed. Slowly.

Through the trees.
Over a log.

Under a branch.
"Here we are!"
said Newton.

"That isn't a pool," said Tessy.
"That's a puddle!"

"What's the difference?" said Newton.
"They both get you wet."

"This can't get me wet!" said Tessy.
"I'm too big!"

Newton got wet. He jumped.
He splashed.

Tessy crossed her arms. She sighed.
She stomped!

Water splashed everywhere.

"You're getting the idea," said Newton.

Tessy had a different idea. It was a windy idea. She put Newton in her bike basket. She put her shoes on the pedals.

Newton had a sleepy idea. He put his nose under his tail. He shut his eyes.

"Here we goooo!" yelled Tessy.

They rocketed down the hill.

"Nooo, go slowwwww!" yelled Newton. He covered his ear holes.

"We are flying!" yelled Tessy.

"I don't flyyyy!" yelled Newton. "It's a chameleon rule!"

The bike stopped.

"You turned *green*!" she said.

"I don't like bike riding. It is too fast. It is not fun. And it makes it impossible to nap!" Newton said.

"I don't like napping. It is too slow. It is so boring. And it makes it impossible to have fun!" said Tessy.

Newton flicked his tongue.

"Why are you sticking your tongue out?" asked Tessy.

"I always stick my tongue out. It's what chameleons do," said Newton.

"It is not nice," said Tessy, crossing her arms.

"That's it!" said Newton, turning brown. "Picnics hurt. I'm losing sleep. And chameleons don't fly! Being friends is not my thing."

Chapter Five

Newton sat on a leaf. He did not look at Tessy.

Tessy sat on a log. She did not look at Newton.

Newton saw a centipede.

Tessy did not see a centipede.

Newton saw the centipede crawl in Tessy's sock.

Tessy felt the centipede crawl in her sock.

"*Eeek!* I do not like centipedes!" screamed Tessy.

Newton's tongue flicked. Gulp. Burp. "Ew. I do not like centipedes either," said Newton.

"You ate the bug, but you did not like it?" asked Tessy.

"Yep," said Newton. "It is what chameleons do."

"It's what friends do," said Tessy.
She gave Newton a finger hug.
Newton turned pink.

"Newton?" said Tessy.

"Yep," said Newton.

"Let's do something that's fun for both of us."

"Not a lot of options," said Newton. "You are a kid. I am a chameleon."

"But we are both friends," said Tessy.

"Maybe we are," said Newton.

"What is fun for you?"
asked Tessy.

"I like to see the sun
go down," said Newton.
"What is fun for you?"

"I like to see the moon come up!"
said Tessy.

Newton crawled onto Tessy's finger.

"Hungry?" said Tessy.

"Yep," said Newton. "But not
for falling grapes."

Tessy smiled. She gave Newton
a cricket.

Newton smiled. He gave Tessy
a cookie.

They sat on the rock. They ate snacks.

"Picnics are fun after all,"
said Newton.

"Rock sitting is fun too," said Tessy.

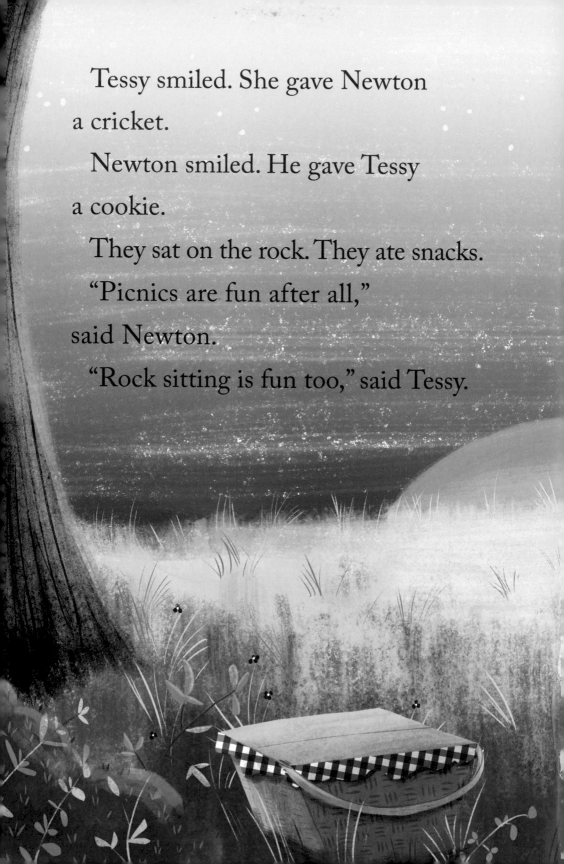

"Look! The sun is going down!"

"Yep," said Newton. "And the moon is coming up."

Tessy and Newton watched the sun and the moon share the sky...together.

Chameleon Facts

Do chameleons really change colors?

Some chameleons do change colors! They have a special way of changing colors that is caused, in part, by their feelings. They change color to reflect the mood they are in.

Some chameleons can only change from brown to green and back again. But other chameleons can turn many colors!

Some chameleons can change colors really fast, in a matter of seconds.

Changing colors can send messages to other chameleons, like warnings. It can help attract another chameleon too.

Another reason chameleons change colors is because of light and temperature. A chameleon that is cold might change to a darker color to absorb more heat. This will warm him up.